GOOD SPORTS

C.J. SLINGER, LEFT WINGER

By K.A. Robertson
Illustrated by Karl West

Rourke
Educational Media
rourkeeducationalmedia.com

www.rourkeeducationalmedia.com

Edited by: Keli Sipperley
Cover layout and interior layout by: Rhea Magaro-Wallace
Cover and interior illustrations by: Karl West

Library of Congress PCN Data

C.J. Slinger, Left Winger / K.A. Robertson
(Good Sports)
ISBN 978-1-64369-045-2 (hard cover)(alk. paper)
ISBN 978-1-64369-093-3 (soft cover)
ISBN 978-1-64369-192-3 (e-Book)
Library of Congress Control Number: 2018956035

Printed in the United States of America,
North Mankato, Minnesota

Table of Contents

Chapter One
Ready or Not

I'm C.J. Slinger. I play ice
hockey. I don't know all the
rules yet. But I like cheering
for my team from the bench!

"Are you ready for the game?" Riley asks. She is chewing gum. It smells like cotton candy.

"I think so. What does *offsides* mean again?"

Riley blows a bubble. I pop
it. We laugh.

"That's when you skate
into the other team's **zone**
before the **puck** is in there,"
she says.

"Got it," I say. I don't really
"got it." But I am sure I won't
be playing much anyway.

The third graders play the most. I am only in first grade. I have lots of time to learn.

Chapter Two
Uh-Oh

"Bad news, team," Coach Goats says.

I look up from lacing my ice skates.

Our goalie, Robby, sneezes.
He scratches under his nose
with his glove.

"The first and second lines are out sick today," Coach Goats says. "Seems everyone has got the pukes. That means you guys will have to skate most of the game. C.J., you start at **left wing**."

Uh-oh, I think. I open my mouth. No words come out. I close it.

"You do know what left wing is, don't you?" Coach Goats asks.

"Um, yes," I say. *No, my brain reminds me. Thanks, brain.*

"Okay, team, who are we?" Coach Goats yells.

"The Blobfish!" we yell back.

"And what are we going to do today?"

"Win!" my teammates yell.

I do not yell. I'm trying to
remember why I wanted to
be on this team. And also
I am wondering why our
school **mascot** is a blobfish.

Chapter Three
Game On

It's game time. My hands feel sweaty in my gloves. I think I might get the pukes. I want to tell Coach Goats I can't play.

Principal Ponytail taps the microphone. He clears his throat. Then he says, "Play ball!"

Principal Ponytail says "play ball" before every game. Even checkers.

The **referee** drops the
puck. Riley wins the faceoff!
She passes the puck to me.

I catch it with my stick. I take off. I skate fast! I am C.J. Slinger, left winger! I got this!

My lungs tickle with icy air.

I skate toward the goalie. I

shoot the puck.

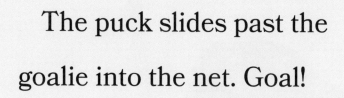

The puck slides past the
goalie into the net. Goal!

I pump my arms in the air.

"Woohoo!" I yell. It is quiet.

Too quiet.

I look around. My teammates stare at me. The other team cheers.

"Wrong net," I groan. I want to go home. I want to change schools.

My teammates pat my

back.

"It's okay," Robby says.

"That was a sweet goal!"

"Let's score one on the other goalie next time," Coach Goats yells. He laughs. I laugh too.

"Nice one," Riley says.

"Ready to play?"

"Ready," I say.

Bonus Stuff!

Glossary

goalie (GOH-lee): A player who guards the net to keep the other team from scoring.

left wing (left wing): An offensive player that plays on the left side of the ice.

mascot (MAS-kaht): An animal or symbol that represents a sports team.

puck (puhk): A hard, round, flat piece of rubber used in ice hockey.

referee (ref-uh-REE): An official who supervises a sports match to make sure the players obey the rules.

zone (zohn): In hockey, there are three zones. Each team has a zone where their goalie guards the net. Players try to score in their opponent's zone. The middle zone is the neutral zone.

Discussion Questions

1. What emotions do you think C.J. was feeling when he got out on the ice?

2. Do you think these emotions caused him to get mixed up when the game started?

3. Do you think C.J.'s teammates showed good sportsmanship?

Activity:
Mini Hockey Sticks

You can use these mini hockey sticks to play table hockey with mini marshmallows or raisins! Make sure you have an adult's permission to use the scissors.

Supplies
- wood craft sticks or ice pop sticks
- glue
- markers or colored tape
- scissors

Directions
1. Cut the bottom third of a craft or ice pop stick at an angle. This will be the blade of your hockey stick.

2. Glue the blade to the bottom of another craft or ice pop stick.

3. When the glue is dry, use markers to color bands at the top of the stick and around the blade to look like hockey tape. You can also put thin strips of colored tape around the top and blade.

Writing Prompt

Write a hockey song! Using the glossary words from the story, make up a song about hockey. Sing it to the tune of "Row, Row, Row Your Boat" or "Three Blind Mice."

About the Author

K.A. Robertson is a writer, editor, and hockey fan. She has two sons who play ice hockey in sunny Tampa, Florida. She loves going from the cold rink to the warm beach!

About the Illustrator

Karl West lives and works from a studio on the small island of Portland in Dorset, England. His dogs, Ruby and Angel, lie under his desk while he works, snoring away.